SECRET AGENT MAN

S.A.M. is digging for the Lost City of Raisins...

He is tracking down the treacherous green spitting bug,

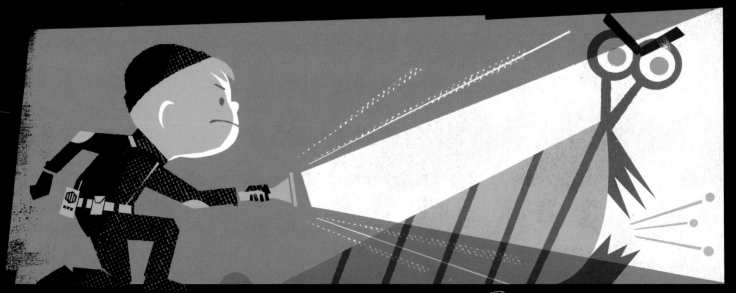

balancing on high places,

and stealing home.

K. is hanging out clouds.
"You need new shoes," says K.

To my three wonderful children,
who all learned to tie their shoes,
eventually
T. W.-J.

To Mum and Dad
B. W.

First published 2016 by Walker Books Ltd
87 Vauxhall Walk, London SE11 5HJ

2 4 6 8 10 9 7 5 3 1

Text © 2016 Tim Wynne-Jones

Illustrations © 2016 Brian Won

The right of Tim Wynne-Jones and Brian Won to be identified as author and illustrator
respectively of this work has been asserted by them in accordance with the Copyright,
Designs and Patents Act 1988

This book has been typeset in Caecilia Bold

Printed in China

British Library Cataloguing in Publication Data:
a catalogue record for this book is available
from the British Library

ISBN 978-1-4063-6844-4

www.walker.co.uk

FSC
MIX
Paper from
responsible sources
FSC™ C020056

SECRET AGENT MAN

GOES SHOPPING FOR SHOES

TIM WYNNE-JONES

illustrated by BRIAN WON

WALKER BOOKS
AND SUBSIDIARIES
LONDON • BOSTON • SYDNEY • AUCKLAND

S.A.M. and K. go shopping for shoes.

"I can't decide whether I want rocket shoes
or vanishing shoes," says S.A.M.

"I'll be right with you, madam," says Shoe Store Man.

"That's K.," says S.A.M. "Short for Kay."

Shoe Store Man looks shifty.
"Search him," says S.A.M.

S.A.M. tries on lots of shoes.

"I'll take the ones with tiger stripes," says S.A.M.

"I'll have the same," says K.

S.A.M. watches Shoe Store Man tie his laces.
One bow, two bows. Over, under, and pull them tight.

"How about lunch?" says K.

"ROAR",
says S.A.M.

He orders the double cheese burger with a side
of snakes and an electron milkshake.

"We are matching tigers," he says.

"ROAR," says K.

35

On the bus home, someone tries to steal the Plans for World Domination.

"Oh, no, you don't," says S.A.M.

"Phew! That was close," says K.

"I feel woozy," says S.A.M. "Someone must have slipped something bad into my milkshake."

"I'd suggest forty winks of sleep," says K.

"Make that twenty-seven winks," says S.A.M.
"I've got an important meeting."

He watches K. untie his shoelaces. One bow.
Then the other.

S.A.M. dreams of beautiful poisonous butterflies
and dangerous inflatable frogs.

His important meeting goes well.

"These are the Plans for World Domination," he tells his Team of Expert Spies. "Decode them and have the results on my desk by three."

"Will do," says Agent Wolf.

"Yes, sir," says Agent Ted.

"Three on the dot," says Agent Pig.

"Good," says S.A.M., and goes looking for K.

Chamber of
Silence.

She's not in
the Holding Cell
of Despair.

She's not in
the Torture
Chamber ...

"Uh-oh," he says. Quickly he puts on his new shoes and runs as fast as a tiger to the rescue.

K. is bringing in the clouds.

"Let me help!" shouts S.A.M.

They sit and watch the storm, drinking steaming mugs of lava topped with dollops of pearls.

"Lucky my Team of Expert Spies warned me about the storm," says S.A.M.

"T.O.E.S," says K.

"Right," says S.A.M. "We're ready for anything."

"Good," says K.

S.A.M. looks at his new tiger shoes. They look very excited and proud.

"S.A.M.," says K, "did you tie your own shoelaces?"

"ROAR!"

says S.A.M.